W9-ARC-165

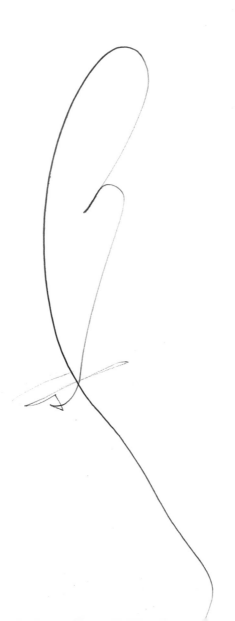

Mike and the Snow Dragon

adapted by Daphne Prendergrass
illustrated by Hit Entertainment

Ready-to-Read

Simon Spotlight
New York London Toronto Sydney New Delhi

MCL FOR
NEPTUNE CITY
PUBLIC LIBRARY

SIMON SPOTLIGHT

An imprint of Simon & Schuster Children's Publishing Division

1230 Avenue of the Americas, New York, New York 10020

This Simon and Spotlight edition September 2014

© 2014 Hit (MTK) Limited. Mike the Knight™ and logo and Be a Knight, Do It Right!™ are trademarks of Hit (MTK) Limited.

All rights reserved, including the right of reproduction in whole or in part in any form.

SIMON SPOTLIGHT, READY-TO-READ, and colophon are registered trademarks of Simon & Schuster, Inc.

For information about special discounts for bulk purchases, please contact Simon & Schuster Special Sales at 1-866-506-1949 or business@simonandschuster.com.

The Simon & Schuster Speakers Bureau can bring authors to your live event. For more information or to book an event contact the Simon & Schuster Speakers Bureau at 1-866-248-3049 or visit our website at www.simonspeakers.com.

Manufactured in the United States of America 0814 LAK

10 9 8 7 6 5 4 3 2 1

ISBN 978-1-4814-1909-3 (hc)

ISBN 978-1-4814-1908-6 (pbk)

ISBN 978-1-4814-1910-9 (eBook)

Mike the Knight
loved winter.
He was excited to play
in the snow!

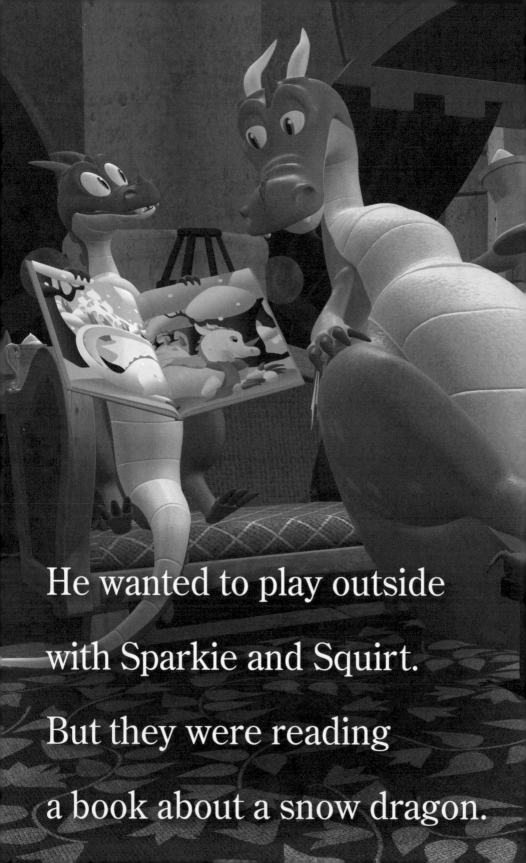

He wanted to play outside
with Sparkie and Squirt.
But they were reading
a book about a snow dragon.

It had an orange horn.

It lived in the woods.

Sparkie and Squirt

wanted to stay inside.

They had never played
in the snow!

Mike wanted to help
his friends get used
to the snow!

He took out his sword.

There was a carrot!

"How will I use this?"

Mike wanted to know.

They all went outside.

Sparkie liked the ice!

Then a pile of snow
fell on Squirt.

"I am cold!" he cried.

Next they went on a walk.

Sparkie liked the snow.

Squirt was cold and wet.

He wanted to go home.

Mike told Squirt,

"Maybe the snow dragon

lives in Tall Tree Woods!"

Squirt wanted to meet

the snow dragon!

They did not find a
snow dragon in the woods.

"Look!" Mike pointed.

"Snow dragon tracks!"

"It must be close!"

Squirt said.

Sparkie was not fooled.
"Mike, those are my
footprints," Sparkie said.

Mike felt bad about lying.

Then he heard a yell.

Mike slid to the rescue

on his shield!

Squirt was stuck!

"Are you okay?"

asked Mike.

"No!" Squirt cried.
"I am cold and wet.
And I did not find
the Snow Dragon!"

Mike felt awful.

"I am sorry, but I lied.

Snow dragons are not real."

"Now I will never see a snow dragon!" cried Squirt.

Mike felt even worse.

Then he had an idea.

They piled up snow.

They used stones for eyes.

They made a horn with
the carrot from the sword!

They made a snow dragon!

Squirt had so much fun that

he forgot he was cold.

Mike was happy.

His friends liked the snow!

They raced to the castle

to warm up.

It was a fun day!

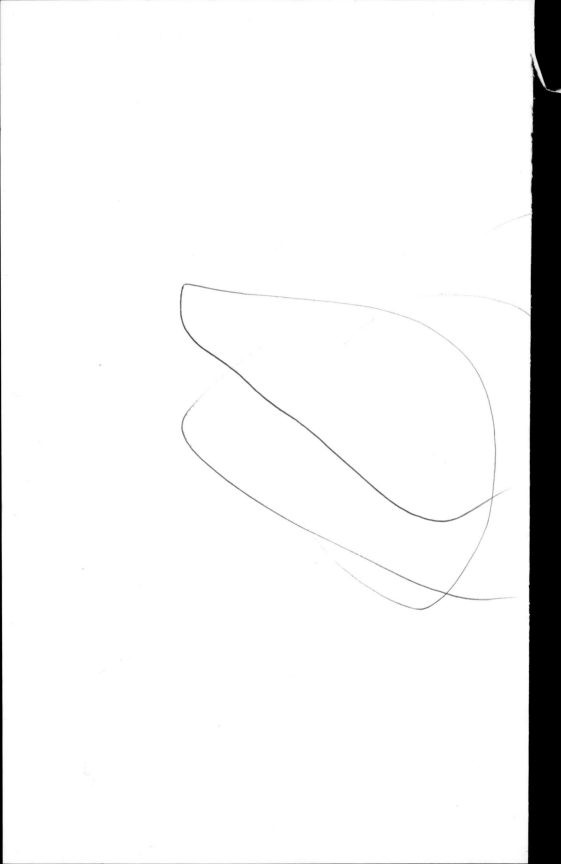